LITTLE RED RISING HOOD

CLARISSA KAE

CARPE VITAM
· PRESS LLC ·

AUTHOR'S NOTE

Although many of the injustices of medieval Wales are true, the town and characters I've written are fictional. The eternal truth that war is won on the backs of women is, and always will be, true.

CHAPTER 1

$\mathcal{L}$ady Alys Ysgarlad

THE MOMENT the moon cast enough light through the narrow windows of the castle, Alys crept down the winding staircase of ancient stone and down into the abandoned dungeon. Light on her feet, she fluttered across the stone floor to the corner. She cast one last glance over her shoulder. Like every other night, no sounds echoed in the dark behind her. Grandmother would be at her window, her eyes and ears peeled for the man servants of the castle and the small village. Always watching—mistrusting—Alys had learned from the best.

Alys kneeled and pulled up the wood panel she'd painted to look like stone. In one movement, she jumped inside and lowered the doorway behind her—enveloping her in full darkness. Thin, steep stairs looped around before the corridor led to underneath the stables. Her shoulders bumped the sides, and her legs ached with the familiar crouch. Only a small frame could maneuver the low ceiling and cramped tunnel with any amount of speed. No matter how many times Alys had come, her heart pounded with fear—and excitement. There was a strength, a burning of righteous fury that grew with each shadowed step.

Out of habit, she kept a hand out in front of her, the other hand on the rugged stone wall as she blindly made her way. Alys never took a candle—the risk of being found too great. At the end of the tunnel, she felt for the notches carved into the stone, grasped the faint edges with her fingertips, and began climbing. Thank goodness she'd never had to attempt this in a dress. She pushed through the panel in the corner of the barn's tack room. The crisp air stole her breath, her pulse racing ever faster. She grabbed the bow and arrows hidden in a loose panel of a stall, tucked the board back into the wall, and rushed onward.

Scurrying under the rising moon, she was at her post where the creek turned under the road, marking the edge of the woods. The wind rustled the branches and the creatures stirred the leaves on the forest floor. The gentle sounds of the night were deafening against the pounding of Alys's heart.

From the castle, her grandmother would be watching—waiting in relative safety looking over the women of the village and their rebellion.

Hidden from view, Alys waited for the signal. In the upper most window of the inn down the road, a lantern flickered to life. The tax collector had finally arrived. They'd been planning since word of his arrival had first reached the village.

The lantern died, the next round of lights would show where he was staying. Two lanterns were lit. He was staying at Cadoc Inn. She waited another moment. A simple tax collector at Cadoc. Her pulse dulled to an easy rhythm. He was just one of a long list of lazy men who'd come with greedy eyes and empty thoughts. They would only need a few women tonight. He'd be outwitted and sent on his way.

Alys hid the bow and arrows underneath the bridge—this was a simple job. Being caught with a bow and arrows, and dressed as a man, would be anything but simple. Keeping to the shadows, Alys met a dozen other hidden figures at the inn's barn. She held up a hand and stretched out her fingers, indicating the need for only five women. Wordless, several women disappeared into the dark. Three women went inside the barn. They would steal the tax collector's horse and saddle out from under the groom's nose, while Alys and one other would see to the tax collector.

Alys watched, a lump forming in her throat. It'd been nearly four years of sneaking out in the dead of night to take care of the village. The women knew what to do without Alys uttering a word. She should be swollen with pride, not feeling a sense of dread...and sadness.

In the deepest part of her heart, she wasn't truly sad. She was angry. The fury bright against the darkest part of her livid soul.

Her father was the Marcher lord. He should be here defending the villagers, not drinking himself into oblivion on bended knee with the king. This town—and the entire Welsh country—would be won on the backs of women, not on the pride of stubborn men.

Alys placed a hand on the nearest woman, a tattered cloak pulled around her face. The woman nodded and followed Alys to the inn's servant entrance. The tip of the woman's brunette plait fell forward. *Catrin.*

"Your hair," Alys whispered.

Untying her cloak, Catrin tucked her plait behind her neck. Three knocks pounded on the other side of the door. Eyes wide, Catrin scurried to pull up her makeshift hood.

Alys stepped in front of her, whispering over her shoulder. "Hurry."

The door opened, revealing a hooded figure. Alys sighed in relief. There'd been far too many whispers of their adventures. It would only take one witness to see Catrin with a fellow hooded figure to start questioning all the women. In truth, if any of the villagers were to pay attention, every woman would be identified. Even now, the slip of a woman who'd opened the door for Alys and Catrin was easily marked. She was the inn keeper's daughter, the clue lying in the twice-patched boots. The patch was made of the same material as the bedding—just as Catrin's shawl was made from the same grain burlap her family wore. Abandoned by fathers and husbands, the entire village was drowning in poverty. While the men were off becoming heroes, the women had begun ruling from the shadows.

The inn keeper's daughter kept her chin down. Warmth wrapped around Alys. This was a girl not yet twelve. How she had heard of the hooded women, Alys didn't care. Another soul added to their army was a win.

With Catrin on her heels, Alys followed the girl up the steep stairs, careful to stay light on her toes. The girl stopped at the first door at the top of the stair case, lighting spilling into the dark hallway.

A hand on the door, Alys paused. "He's been given a drink?"

The daughter nodded and opened the door. The tax collector lay on the floor, his back propped against the wall. Staring at his hand, he hummed a song, his eyes glazed.

This would be even simpler than Alys had thought.

"Say nothing," Alys whispered to the girl and Catrin. Stepping into the room, Alys pointed to the bags strewn across the floor before kneeling before the tax collector. His official ring blinked at Alys in the candlelight. Catrin went to work, emptying his bags on the bed, piling documents into one bag, coin in the other. The rest, he could keep.

"It's beautiful isn't it?" The man showed his hand to Alys, beaming like a toddler. "I made it m'self." Spittle dripped from his lips as his words slurred together.

Pulling the dwale mixture from her pocket, Alys placed the man's hand around the small vassal, guiding the liquid to his mouth. She'd learned long ago that men were much more cooperative if they believed their own hand was doing the work.

Gulping at the liquid, he grunted. Alys pulled back, but he ripped the vassal from her hand and greedily drank the rest of it. The fool would be sick for days instead of only one night. Together the women stood over him as his eyes drooped and his body relaxed. The vassal fell from his hand. Catrin picked up the vassal while Alys poured oil over his hand. Pulling and twisting, Alys stole the official ring from his pudgy finger.

With the bags stuffed with documents and collected coin, Catrin poured pigs blood along his arms and legs. He would wake in a stupor with blood on his hands and not a coin to his name. He would scurry away like the tax collector before him.

A flash of metal caught Alys's hand—Catrin held a knife in her hand, her eye on the tax collector, her jaw clenched in anger.

"No." Alys stepped in front of the slumbering man. "We do not harm," she whispered.

Catrin gripped the knife, eyes still fixed on him.

Her heart sinking, Alys knew the scars on Catrin's face and was haunted by her own memories of her father's heavy hand.

"He may be fat with the king's spoils, but this man has never harmed you," she tried again.

Catrin's shoulders sank. She slipped the knife back into her pocket and picked up the bags. Not waiting for Alys, she disappeared into the corridor. Stealing was one thing, but if men were to be killed...the king may take notice. He'd send an army once before. The country was still grappling with the loss.

Alys surveyed their handiwork before following Catrin. Whispering to the girl, she said, "Meet us at the barn for your share."

Without a candle, Alys could almost see the anticipation of the women before entering the inn's barn. Catrin had already divvied the coin, two piles left waiting for Alys and the girl.

"No," Alys offered quietly and held up the ring to the small audience. "One more to add—"

"No." Catrin's voice came hard.

Silence filled the barn in a heavy rush.

"No." Using her boot, Catrin toed the pile of coin. "That is all you ever say."

Alys stepped forward and pulled the hood off her head. "I've no child with hungry eyes. No husband sent off to the king's war. No father bent in shame." She waved to the pile. "Take the coins."

"You've a cold castle and an empty heart." Catrin bent and scooped some coins in her hand before glancing back up at Alys. "You've more a reason to take your share than the rest of us."

Cold castle. Alys swallowed the rising emotion. *Empty heart.* These good women thought she was robbed as they were, but she knew the truth. Her father was a Marcher lord, the roof over her head was stolen from a native Welsh lord and given to him. She vowed to give everything to the deserving. "I'd rather warm your bellies than my father's castle." She held up the tax collector's ring. "And my heart bleeds for no man."

The inn keeper's daughter rushed in. "King men," she gasped. "Another group of king men have arrived."

CHAPTER 2

*G*areth Blaidd

IN THE DEAD OF NIGHT, Gareth arrived at the edge of Tenby. A breeze teased the branches, but all Gareth felt was the rush of longing. And nostalgia. On other either side of the small village were two castles— the southern estate should have been his destination, but the northern castle had once held his heart.

Every summer of his youth, Gareth was shipped to his uncle's castle on the southern tip of town, its land bordering Ysgarlad land. It was at his uncle's side that Gareth had learned to track both man and beast. He'd also learned to move soundless through the woods—a talent the King of England had decided to acquire.

The sound of the carriage pulled Gareth back to the present, turning his thoughts heavy. His last conversation in the village had been with Lord Gower, Lady Alys's father. His voice had boomed and the vein on his neck bulged but his message had been clear—Gareth was banned from Ysgarlad land.

Before the carriage could stop, Gareth guided his horse forward.

He'd been grateful the king's appointed man preferred the carriage. The feel of a breeze and the movement of the horse was a welcome distraction to anything a king man could say. They descended toward Cadoc Inn. There was less for the king man to confiscate at the inn than at his family's castle—the other resting place of choice for the men sent this way.

It'd been years since his uncle had died, but Gareth couldn't bring himself to visit. He'd inherited the small castle but could not bear to look across the way at the Ysgarlad estate without bitter regret.

"There's not a light on." Harold Rhode's voice came from behind Gareth.

"It's late."

"It's an inn."

"These are honest people. Simple people." Gareth led his horse around back toward the barn.

"Who don't know how to greet weary travelers," Harold continued complaining but his words faded behind Gareth in the darkness.

Gareth slid open the barn door, pausing. A feeling of being watched came over him. He slowly closed his eyes. Like a nagging mother, Harold had picked apart every word and every moment Gareth had spent in the presence of his fellow Welshman. He continually looked for weakness and searched for motives in Gareth's employment to the king—there was only one.

Brushing down his horse should not have warranted another supervision moment with the gruff Englishman. Slowly, Gareth removed the saddle and fed his horse. He didn't dare leave his saddle in the barn, not with the rumors of thieves. He waited for Harold to appear, barbs at the ready, but clearly the man didn't wish to sully himself with the animals.

Not until Gareth left the barn did the prickling sensation up the back of his neck return. He glanced about and wondered if someone lurked beyond in the woods. He smiled, a memory of teaching Alys how to climb trees brought a rare burst of joy. He would see her while he was here—the village was too small for them to never cross paths.

He swallowed.

Twice he looked back, certain someone was watching him and each time, another memory—an image of Alys's mischievous smile—appeared in his mind. Long after he'd bid a stiff good night to Harold and laid on his bed, the sound of Alys's voice echoed in his ears... *Wolf.*

Surrounded by memories, Gareth tossed and turned. Not a few hours later, a pounding on the door had Gareth groaning.

"Get up." Harold's clipped voice echoed down the hall as he knocked again.

The night sky had begun to lighten, morning was near. Gareth had spent most of the night traveling and couldn't even rest before facing another Harold complaint. Stifling a grunt, Gareth opened the door, still dressed from their travels.

Tall and thin, Harold stood there, a hand still lifted in the air from knocking and his face in an ever-present pinched scowl. "We've a problem."

"Can it wait until morning?"

"A tax collector was attacked." Brown hair, brown eyes and a sodden complexion did nothing for the plain, wretched Harold Rhode. When Gareth didn't respond, Harold narrowed his eyes and stepped forward. "Our orders are to—"

"To investigate a rebellion—"

"To *quell* the rebellion." Lowering his voice, Harold came within inches of Gareth and looked down his nose—a feat considering Gareth was several inches taller. "You are in the employ of your king. Do not forget your place."

"Employ?" Gareth shook his head. "That implies I had a choice."

Harold smiled, his front tooth chipped from an ambush a few towns back. "Your ancestral lands for your cooperation."

And there was the one reason Gareth did what he did for the king. Gareth was Welsh by birth, raised half the year in London, the other half at his uncle's side. His family had played nice with the volatile throne of England, but their loyalty was always by blood, never by crown. At the start of every Welsh rebellion, there was a Blaidd relative. England thought that keeping the Blaidd patriarch under golden

9

chains in London would temper their Welsh pride. And now, Gareth's ancestral lands were dangled in front of him to ensure cooperation.

Harold smirked, waiting for Gareth to put on his boots. "You're getting a better deal than any other Welshman."

"A deal with the devil himself," Gareth mumbled as he shoved on his second boot.

Before Harold could sneer, his footman—a boy just shy of thirteen—bounded down the corridor. "The man's babbling about in the street."

Gareth hung back, following from a distance as Harold ran with the boy at his side. The longer Gareth took to see the tax collector, the fewer complaints he'd have to endure. He descended the stairs and was met with silence. Harold and the boy were already out on the street, but the bar was still lined with men, beards gray and eyes filled with contempt. He couldn't blame them. Word would spread that he'd betrayed his own kind. They wouldn't know the reason nor would they care. Just as he reached the door, he heard a murmured, "Never thought a wolf would stab us in the back."

Wolf. Gareth kept walking, his childhood nickname echoing in his head. The sing-song accents of the Welsh used to sooth his soul, not remind him of the noose around his neck. He'd bartered with a greedy king, promising his talent of tracking to keep the village safe.

The moment Gareth left the inn, the conversations of the men rose. A stab of grief pricked him. At his uncle's side, Gareth would have been teased and brought into barrel hugs. Proclamations of how much he'd grown would be followed by the men clapping each other on the back.

In the center of the street was a man crawling on his hands and knees, dirt and blood covering his trousers and sleeves. Gareth came closer, unsure he could believe his eyes in the dim light of the early morning.

The sun had yet to cast its first rays, but Harold stood over the man, shouting.

"You're going to wake the entire town," Gareth pointed out. He glanced back the inn. Well, whomever hadn't spent the night at the bar of the inn.

The stench of the man had Gareth breathing through his mouth.

"This is no tax collector," Harold growled.

Bending over the man, Gareth sniffed. The man smelled like a butcher shop. "Your name, sir?"

Grinning, saliva ran down the man's mouth. He held up his hand and giggled.

"That's a fine hand," Gareth murmured and rubbed his fingers on the man's trouser, the blood dried. He sniffed his fingers. It had to be the blood of an animal.

Harold turned to the boy. "Do you know the name of this man?"

"No, sir." The boy kept his head low. "The innkeeper said he arrived night before last. Came crawling down the stairs an hour ago. Drunk. Singing."

Gareth didn't hear the boy, childhood memories stole his focus. He shook his head. HE needed to become mast of his mind, this was just another town. He had to forget he was investigating the town that raised him.

Grabbing the man's chin, Harold shouted, "What is your name?"

"He's too drunk." Gareth straightened to his full height. Between the drunk man's breath and the animal blood, there was something suspicious going on. Yes, tax collectors often threw their weight around for favors...but this...this was something else. Something *more*.

"If this man is truly a collector, he'll be removed from his post." Narrowing his eyes, Harold glanced up the road and back at Gareth. "If there's been foul play, then I'll not hesitate to punish."

Gareth brushed his hands on his trousers. "I would expect nothing less." He'd played the part of dutiful tracker—but could not, would not, help any of the villagers enter Harold's crosshairs. Gareth had watched one too many homes confiscated in the name of the crown. This little town had fought famine and territorial wars between England and Wales. They didn't need another unfair punishment. He would have to tread carefully.

11

The sky lightened further, and several men slipped out of the bar —most likely to snatch a few hours' sleep before beginning their day. Gareth sighed. He couldn't blame them for finding solace where they could. A place to forget about the state of their existence for a while.

"Search his room—" Harold stopped at the sound of horses running.

Up the road a cloud of dust formed. A moment later four horses appeared. As they came closer, the figures became clearer. Leading the group was a large black horse with feathering on the legs, but all Gareth could focus on was the woman riding it. Her red hair waved in the wind as her horse cantered. *Alys.*

Surrounded by her footmen, Alys halted her horse before the supposed tax collector. In one graceful movement, her skirts swinging around her, she dismounted and peered down at the man completely unaware of Harold and Gareth. She wore no gloves—Gareth's eyes flicked to her hand. No ring.

In a moment, Gareth was pulled back in time when he'd pleaded with her father for her hand. Gareth had helped Alys into the house. He'd stolen a kiss and promised her forever. Lord Gower had laughed and sneered in Gareth's face, telling him Alys was destined for an English nobleman not a Welsh-born country boy.

"Am I to believe you are Lady Alys Ysgarlad?" Harold's voice yanked Gareth back to the moment.

Alys arched an eyebrow at Harold, her dark eyes growing hard. "That is the rumor."

Harold folded his arms on his chest. His patience was thin on a good day. "It appears there are a great many rumors here."

Turning from Harold, she lifted her chin at Gareth. "What could possibly be so important to summon the Great Wolf from the King's war?"

She'd barely given him a glance—believing him to be a traitor like the rest of Tenby.

"Great Wolf?" Harold chuckled, his eye flicking between Alys and Gareth. "Gareth is no wolf."

Alys didn't reply. She bent over the man. Forever a contradiction, she wore the same pearl necklace her mother once wore. She could fight like a street urchin but wear an expensive heirloom. This was Alys Ysgarlad, kind and cruel, fire and ice. "He's been hired to track, yes?" Her gaze flickered to him briefly, and his heart lurched at the familiar shape of her. "Like a predator, I'm sure he can see the weakness." She turned and stood before Harold. "Which is why the king has need of him."

Harold puffed out his chest. "The king has need of no one."

A wry smile played on her lips. "And yet"—she waved to the man on the street—"the king has sent a tax collector."

* * *

HAROLD SCOWLED over their morning meal. "How would the women know so quickly that something was amiss?"

A corner of Gareth's mouth turned upward. "Word travels fast in a place such as this."

"Hmpf." Harold took another large bite of bread.

Gareth could only stare at their meal and feel as if it were stolen rather than paid for.

While a piece of him had ached for home, for Tenby, another part of him knew he wouldn't be welcomed here. Maybe not ever.

For now, he had to learn of the happenings here before Harold—and then find a way to appease the man and send him back to London. How Gareth planned to do that when he would get no cooperation from the town?

He had yet to figure that out. As Harold continued to spew nonsense theories, Gareth replayed in his mind the determined look of Alys as she'd cantered up the street, dismounted, and took in the scene. Pride swelled in him. Her fierce determination and strength had not faded.

CHAPTER 3

*L*ady Alys Ysgarlad

DRESSED as a man in trousers and a dark hood, Alys sat under her bedroom window and waited for the moon to rise, allowing enough light for the women to work. A waning moon now, which meant their days would be numbered and then all work would need to come to a halt. Lanterns and candles would be far easier to notice than women dressed as men, clinging to the shadows.

The door behind her softly opened and her grandmother entered. They'd made small talk in front of the servants at dinner. Both women had watched the man servants send letters to London. Men who were paid to spy on Alys by her father.

Or rather, her legal father.

"There are rumors," her grandmother whispered, her voice filled with worry.

"There are always rumors." Alys didn't look at the old woman. She didn't need to. Lady Ysgarlad, as she was stilled called by the villagers, was a woman who'd seen her husband and son fall to an English sword.

"Gareth has returned."

Leaning into the stone wall, Alys kept her gaze on the dark sky outside. "Not to us."

"He's not staying at the Blaidd estate." Her grandmother stepped closer, her footsteps silent. She was like a ghost, able to flit in and out of rooms without a sound. "He's at the inn."

"With a king man called Harold Rhode." The words were acid on her tongue. She'd learned of Gareth's betrayal months ago. He'd given her pretty promises years before, but like most men from England, he'd turned his back on her. He might have been born a Welshman, but he behaved like a horrid English gent.

"So I've heard." Grandmother allowed herself a soft sigh.

Alys refused to face her. By the lilt in her voice, the old woman had more information on Harold, or perhaps even Gareth, but Alys couldn't stomach it. Not tonight. Tonight, she would have to poach for hours—the only way to fill the starving bellies of the Tenby. It'd be all the more difficult with another king man breathing down their necks. She needed to focus on the plan ahead not wallow in broken promises. Her village would go hungry if she did not.

"Do not pretend you're unaffected, Alys." She stood next to Alys, allowing their shoulders to touch as they peered out the small window. In a moment, Lady Ysgarlad would hand Alys the dagger—the same weapon her grandmother had given her years before. The night she'd started poaching.

With Gareth gone, Alys had become restless. She had defied Lord Gower, asking for leniency for a thieving, starving widow. She'd done the unthinkable and spouted off in front of the servants—she'd been whipped for her indiscretion. Her grandmother had helped nurse her wounds and gave her the ancestral Ysgarlad dagger. Grandmother had whispered in her ear, *our country is run by women. We control the future with our wombs.*

Alys straightened her spine. "I am always affected."

"Your father is set to return as well."

"He's not my father." Alys turned to her grandmother, the once revered Lady Ysgarlad. The silver in the older woman's hair glowed in the moonlight—no longer the deep red that Alys had inherited. "No one knows that better than you."

Her grandmother smiled softly. "You remind me of him."

Him. Alys had been told time and again that she was the spitting image of her father, and his mother, Lady Ysgarlad. Years before, the king had begun marrying Welsh women to English lords, an attempt to bridle the rising rebellion. Alys's father had died fighting against the crown. He was buried before Alys was born, leaving the castle without a man's protection.

"He…" Alys's voice cracked. "He is not here. None of the men are here. My parentage means nothing." With the king's insistence, Lord Gower married Alys's mother before she gave birth—under English law, Alys had become his daughter.

"There's not a drop of English blood in our veins." Lady Ysgarlad held out her arms. "But the crown acknowledges you as an English noble. You might be our salvation."

"The villagers will never recognize me as English. Nor do I want to be recognized as such." She had been called Lady Alys Ysgarlad since birth. Even the servants paid by Lord Gower had refused to call her Lady Alys Gower.

"My dear…" Her grandmother sighed. She tucked a red curl behind Alys's ear. "Your temper is as fiery as your hair." She tilted her head and looked at the window, clearly something weighing on her mind. "You are my granddaughter. I am as proud of you today as I have always been…"

"Speak plainly." Alys's pulse began racing.

"You cannot be arrested as easily as I can." Lady Ysgarlad squeezed Alys's hands. "Nor can you be thrown in jail or lands confiscated like the villagers."

"I'm Welsh."

"If the crown can steal our coin and our daughters, we might as well use their laws for our gain." Lady Ysgarlad's eyes narrowed, her voice hard. "Gareth is not the enemy you think he is."

"Gareth left." Alys checked her boots. She needed something to distract her. Her father—or legal father—had left. Everyone had left her, even her mother. Guilt pricked her. Alys's mother had died giving birth to a stillborn son. Lord Gower had thought the act a purposeful betrayal. Alys's mother could no sooner plan her death or her son's death than a farmer could schedule rain. But Lord Gower had never been accused of being rational.

"Gareth's return is a fact Lord Gower must surely be aware of." Lady Ysgarlad chuckled, a foreign sound in the dark castle. "I've no doubt Lord Gower heard the news and began rushing back."

"Lord Gower knows Gareth left." Alys could still feel the sting. She'd tried sneaking out when Gareth never returned but Lord Gower had caught her. Told her Gareth had snuck out of town in a hurry. *He seemed to be escaping from someone, do you know who? Perhaps a young miss was trying to entrap him?* The words were etched into her memory, the pain as real today as it was years ago. She'd loved Gareth, his easy temperament and steady affection. He had been kind. Strong. And gentle.

And then he was gone.

"Oh, child." Lady Ysgarlad kneeled before Alys. "I've known love. That man didn't leave of his own accord."

"I cannot stay." Alys stood with a snap. She had far more important concerns than a childhood love. "They need me."

"Do not condemn him for one mistake and forget all the good."

Alys nodded, swallowing the lump in her throat. She'd thought about the *good* and the feelings of safety and warmth—she'd thought of nothing else for months after Gareth had left. The tender way he'd pick her up when she'd fallen, foolishly trying to keep up. His patient smile when she'd brag about besting him. The way he'd slow his gait so she could keep up. There were miles and miles of *good* memories. But there was one simple fact. He'd left when she needed him the most.

Only after Gareth had abandoned her did Lord Gower promise her hand to some ancient lord who had the good sense to die before Alys could be shipped off. If Gareth had never left...she shook the thought. She'd played that game. Wondering what could have been had given her nothing but tears.

She scrambled down the stairs and under the tunnel to the stables. Only when she was deep in the woods, clutching her bow and arrow, did the memories leave her be. Hooded figures gathered to her as she made her orders. "Grab only rabbits. With the king man in town we can't risk a deer."

The two smallest women ran for the outer trees with whistles around their neck. By the looks of it, Alys guessed they were the butcher's twins.

From the groans, Alys wasn't the only one disappointed. There were enough women tonight that they could have carried off a deer easily, but truth be told, it wasn't this Harold Rhode that Alys feared. Gareth could track a poacher like a predator. He, like his father before him, was a tracker unlike any ordinary man. He'd earned the nickname *Wolf* for a reason.

With her bow and arrows secure, Alys climbed the nearest trees. She'd want a look out before hunting the rabbits. The king had vowed the woods were his territory and poaching was punishable by death. For centuries Welsh boys earned their manhood by hunting for food in these woods, and now the women of the village would feed their children. With local English leaders like her father off to war, the woods were ripe for the picking.

Silence stole the subtle sounds of night as the poachers made their way deeper into the woods. Alys relaxed against the tree trunk. Straddling the thick branch underneath her, she listened for the sounds of creatures creeping along the foliage. A handful of her arrows landed below her but with each kill, her mind turned back to Gareth. He'd gently place his hand over hers, guiding and teaching her. She'd finally gained control over her awkward limbs, slowly becoming a young woman. She had thought it would take her weeks to convince Gareth to teach her. He hadn't appeared surprised or if he had, he'd kept it hidden. His closeness was a distraction—his face next to hers, his chest to her back. She could hear him breathe and felt the warmth from her skin.

A whistle blew—sounding like a small bird caught in the night. Someone was entering the woods. Scrambling down the tree, Alys filled her bag with the three rabbits and tossed the used arrows under the brush. She would have to collect them another time. The women gathered at the meeting spot, the pile of game growing. Alys tossed her bag of rabbits on the pile just as another whistle went off.

"Take the pile. Get to the barn. I'll stay here and keep them off your scent." Alys ran toward the woods, ignoring the protest from Catrin. The woman had grown more frustrated that Alys never took a portion. Alys lived in a castle where meat and bread were provided. She didn't hunt for herself but for the village. And for her heritage.

The sound of men arguing sent Alys ducking under the brush. Two figures came closer but only one appeared to be speaking.

"You're not telling me the truth." The shorter man's voice was gruff. He circled the larger man and stood before him. "The tax collector had no documents, no money. Nothing was on him except blood."

The larger man said nothing.

"What is it that you're not telling me?" the shorter man demanded. "You know something."

Again the larger man stayed silent. He side stepped the shorter man and kept walking.

"Gareth," the smaller man snapped.

Gareth. Alys hugged her bow against her chest. Of course it would be him. She shouldn't be affected. The memories were far in the past, a lifetime ago. Alys was no longer the eager girl scooping up the bits of wisdom Gareth imparted. Now, she was in the shadows spying on him—learning what she could to stay safe, and to send him back to the king's war.

The men stepped into the moonlight, revealing the shorter man as Harold Rhode, the king man.

"Gareth, I'm speaking to you!" Harold shouted. "Everyone in this village is a suspect. Their game warden is gone—"

"Look around you, Harold." Gareth's smooth voice and easy

cadence caressed Alys's skin. "This village is barely hanging on. The men are off fighting for their rights—"

"There." Harold pointed at Gareth's chest. "Right there. You *sympathize* with them. They're traitors, the lot of them. Their men are fighting our king. *Our* king."

With one swipe, Gareth shoved Harold's hand away. "I'm just a tracker."

"I saw the way you looked at Lady Alys." Harold kicked at the ground. "It would be a shame if she knew just how talented a tracker you are. How many poachers have you caught? How many thieves did you put to death? After all, you're *just a tracker*."

Sinking back under the brush, Alys's clutched her bow ever tighter. The Gareth from her childhood was loyal. Kind. He'd never hand over a fellow countryman.

"How many homes did you ransack in the name of the king?" Gareth's low voice echoed between the trees as he crouched, inspecting the places she'd just walked. He knew someone had been here. He may even know it was her. "How much land did you steal from the Welsh?"

Harold clapped his hands together and bowed. "All thanks to you."

Gareth kept walking.

"I know you lied," Harold called out. "I know you found the boys in Powys."

Gareth stopped, his back to Harold.

"I know the terms of your agreement." Harold chuckled and began clapping again. "You thought the king, the bloody King of England, would spare your little town if you dedicated your life as a tracker." He bent over and slapped his knees, a forced display of humor.

A chill ran down Alys's spine, and her mind went back to the words from her grandmother. *Oh, child. I've known love. That man didn't leave of his own accord.*

Straightening, Harold added, "You lied. Which means I can do what I like to this bloody village."

CHAPTER 4

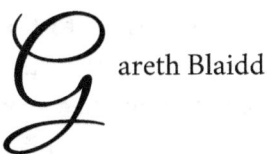areth Blaidd

THE INN WAS QUIET DOWNSTAIRS, the barmaid working in near silence. Gareth could feel her judgement the moment he entered. He wrapped the blame around him like a cloak. She viewed him as the enemy and in truth, she was correct. He was shackled to a king man, the worst sort of betrayal to his Welsh roots.

Rubbing his eyes, he sat at the front, his view on his uncle's estate —or rather, *his* estate. He didn't dare stay there, not with Harold at his side. The man had a reputation for stealing anything of value, claiming it for the king. Gareth had kept careful tabs on everything Harold stole until his list was discovered. Harold had turned from chummy to cruel in an instant.

I know you lied.

Harold's words haunted Gareth, chasing sleep until the early morning hours. He'd only mentioned the one group of boys, but it wouldn't take much for Harold to discover the rest of the lies. For every poacher Gareth had helped Harold find, Gareth had helped several others escape the noose. Wales was starving, and all the king cared about was punishing his Welsh subjects.

Taking in the quiet kitchen, Gareth sighed in relief. For the past few years, Harold had begun each morning with a pounding on Gareth's door. Harold took his assignment of nanny to the extreme. Power did that to men. When Gareth was just a young boy, he'd watched Lord Gower compromise with the villagers and beg for understanding. The moment he married Alys's mother and given the Marcher Lord status from the king, Gower had turned cruel, the final blow when Alys's mother died in childbirth to his son. The villagers retaliated by refusing to call Alys a Gower. In truth, Lady Alys was the spitting image of Lord Ysgarlad, and her mother, widow Lady Ysgarlad. They had the same stubborn set of their chin, the same fiery red hair.

Smiling to himself, Gareth had noticed the arrows tossed to the side in the brush last night. He'd taught Alys how to feather the arrows for smaller prey. Even though he'd not been the one to work the feathers, he'd felt pride nonetheless. Lord Gower would be mad with rage if he knew. Gareth had run into the stout little man only once while in London. He'd made it clear to Gareth that his opinion had not changed—a Welshman would never be welcomed. Alys was to marry an Englishman. With half his life split between London and Tenby, Gareth didn't hold the bitter feelings of either country—until he'd come face to face with gaunt children and desperate mothers.

Gareth waited another moment for Harold before heading to the bar. The poor barmaid froze, appearing unsure of Gareth.

In a low whisper, he said, "You've no reason to trust me."

She rolled her eyes but held her tongue.

"I'd like to interview the tax collector—"

Shaking her head, her eyes went wide.

"Without Harold." He waited for her to pause. "I'm here to help."

She turned away and went back to wiping down the bar.

"Harold believes the villagers are to be punished for how the tax collector was treated."

She paused but didn't meet his gaze.

"I know this county has been stripped of everything. I know this town has been treated unfairly, but I cannot help if I don't know what happened."

"And just how am I to help a traitor?" Her amber eyes glared at him. "I'll not toss over a fellow brother or sister so you can play the hero."

"You wound me." Smiling, he placed a hand on his chest. The darkening of her eyes meant he'd missed the mark. Humor had never been a strength—nor had conversing. Silence was his talent. "I don't need to be a hero. But this town won't survive if Harold proves there's rebellion."

Jutting her chin, she folded her arms. "You've no idea the strength of *our* town. What can and can't survive. We've been doing bloody well for ourselves while you've been gone."

Gareth didn't miss the emphasize on *our* when she spoke of the town. His arrival at a king man's side had destroyed any lingering trust. He wondered how much Alys had spoken of his abrupt departure. He had sent letters but doubted Lord Gower had allowed Alys to read them. The insufferable lord would rather rot than allow his daughter a moment of happiness.

Keeping his gaze down, he offered, "This town raised me. Taught me how to live. How to love. I'd rather take a blade to myself than betray my home."

She opened her mouth as if to speak, but snapped it shut at the sound of footsteps on the staircase. Without another word, she disappeared behind the kitchen wall just as the tax collector descended. His face puffy, he froze at the bottom step, his eyes on Gareth.

Motioning to the door, Gareth asked, "Would you care to join me for a walk?"

"I don't know anything." The swollen parts of his eye gave an eerie, stone-like quality to his stare.

"I'm not here to condemn you."

The man frowned, a feat considering his entire face appeared to be one puffy, swollen mass. "Your friend says otherwise."

Gareth shrugged, knowing very well how Harold ramrodded his interviews. "He is not my friend."

The man relaxed—only a fraction and nodded to the street. "I don't know how I got there."

Guiding the man to a table, Gareth said, "Let's start with your name."

"Tom." He plopped down at the booth, his hands on the table. "I'm no thief."

"Never crossed my mind."

Tom held up a finger. "That's your first lie."

"I do not think you're a thief, Tom." Gareth stretched out on the bench opposite. "I do think you came to this sleepy village to collect taxes, just as the man before you."

Tom folded his hands together, eying Gareth. "I was warned about this place."

"Rumors?" Gareth hoped his question came across as curious and not accusatory. Up and down the Marcher borders were villages just like Tenby, rebellion sprouting up against tax collectors and English landowners—anything resembling the yoke of an English rule.

"Hooded figures come out at night, rob you blind." Tom dropped his gaze to his hands. "I know they gave me something in a drink, I just can't remember who. Or why."

"How do you know?"

"My body doesn't like dwale." He pointed to his swollen face. "Doesn't matter how it's mixed. Any hint of it, and I'm stuffed like a roasted pig."

Gareth nodded to the barmaid working in the kitchen. "Do you think the inn gave you the drink?"

"My head is foggy." Tom sat back on the bench. "I don't remember arriving." He sighed and wiped his hands down face, wincing as his fingers touched his lips. "I don't remember this town. I don't remember how I got here. I only remember the hooded men. There's nothing between, nothing but the little men."

"Little men?"

Waving away the words, Tom shrugged. "Everything is foggy."

The barmaid came to the table and slammed down a plate of biscuits. "Your horse is ready."

"My horse?" Gareth narrowed his eyes at the young woman. "You've touched my horse?"

"The bay." The barmaid spoke only to Tom. "It's saddled and ready for you."

Gareth watched them exchange a look. Tom nodded and began standing. The barmaid had threatened him, but Gareth didn't understand how or why. Gareth had thought the man's horse had run away. That's what they—Harold and he—had been told.

Tom nodded. "I'll be on my way then."

The barmaid flashed a smile to the tax collector only to scowl at Gareth. She rushed off to the kitchen. His brow furrowed in confusion, Tom stood, his eyes following the barmaid's back.

Gareth mirrored his movements, unfolding his enormous frame from under the table. "There's something at play here." He couldn't lead Harold off the scent if he didn't know what had happened.

"I want no part of this." Tom's voice was firm, his eyes hard. "I'm leaving this town, and I won't be back to this forsaken country."

"I'll accompany you."

"No." Tom held up his hand. "I don't want any trouble."

"Trouble is what I'm worried about." Nodding toward the door, Gareth said, "You might be walking into trouble's lap."

Gareth followed Tom to the stables.

In the barn, Tom whispered, "I've been to many a town and the women beg me not to collect. They all have the same complaint in these Welsh towns." He glanced over his shoulder as he greeted his horse. "It's the women."

"The women?" Stifling a chuckle, Gareth patted the horse's neck, a decent animal, nothing fancy enough to steal or smart enough to find its way home. Was this the horse he'd rode in on? Gareth wasn't certain. He was only sure this man would do anything to leave this place.

"Laugh all you want." Tom lead the horse toward the door. "But this is the only town that the women look me in the eye—and it's not a compliment. They're wishing me ill."

CHAPTER 5

$\mathcal{L}$ady Alys Ysgarlad

REACHING the door to her bedroom, Alys nearly collided with her grandmother, her eyes wide and face flushed. Lady Ysgarlad rushed inside the room and whirled around. "Do you have the dagger?"

"Here." Alys pulled the dagger from her pocket. "You weren't in when I came in last—"

Lady Ysgarlad put a finger to her lips and slipped the dagger into her own pocket. Whispering, she guided Alys toward her bed. "Get in and pretend you are ill."

Obedient, Alys did as she was bid.

"Lord Gower has sent his squire." Lifting the blankets, her grandmother helped Alys under the covers. "He's been sent to spy."

"And the reason I'm ill?" Though, it was clear it had something to do with the squire—as if the servants weren't spying enough already.

"He wishes to speak to you."

"What of the dagger?"

"It is better you know nothing." A wicked grin crept along Lady Ysgarlad's face. Tucking the blanket around Alys, Grandmother leaned forward and lowered her voice to barely above a whisper, "The tax collector was given back his horse. He's returning to London. He'll not speak of what happened, if he could remember anything."

Alys made sure everyone abided by her grandmother's rules. "I am the only woman who spoke. And even then, not until the collector or poacher has had some dwale—the latest collector was no exception."

Her grandmother nodded, her eyes bright. "Word is spreading."

"How can this be good?" Alys whispered as Grandmother continued to wrap her in blankets. "We take such pains to be secretive, and you're giddy at the crown knowing of our rebellion?"

Grandmother's eyes darkened, but a corner of her mouth betrayed her excitement. "The blame lies at Lord Gower's feet."

"Gareth." Alys sat up. "Is this Gareth's doing?"

Lady Ysgarlad gently pushed her back down. "That man would injure himself before he'd hurt your family."

Grandmother's loyalty to someone who had so fully betrayed his people made little sense. "He works for the king now," she said. "Harold was threatening him last night."

Just as grandmother opened her mouth to speak, a soft knock was followed by the child of the cook. "Sorry, miss...m'lady..." she whispered. "There's visitors."

Alys immediately stood.

"You're ill," Grandmother gave her a pointed look.

Coughing into her fist, Alys bent over and pretended to be ill. She could obey her grandmother and still investigate who had come to the castle. "I'll wear a warm shawl," she said as she snatched one off the top of her bed.

"You'll need to do more than that to be convincing," Lady whispered as she started for the door.

Alys quickly pulled her hair over a shoulder and created a messy plait, which hung to her waist.

Following the cook and her grandmother down the corridor, the voices grew louder.

"My horse has disappeared!" A man shouted.

Alys and Lady Ysgarlad exchanged a questioning look as they made their way down the wide staircase. The moment they came into the parlor, Alys froze.

The Squire—Alys refused to use his name—stood as if posed in front of the fireplace. This was not his castle. Not his place. And yet... her and grandmother were helpless to prevent him from strutting about as if he were the lord of the castle.

But worse yet, Gareth stood next to the squire, Harold Rhode pacing behind them. Memories of the last time Gareth was in her home, had Alys' face draining of color.

"I don't see how this could have happened," the squire said as his brows pulled down—his face showing every mark of disdain.

Alys fought the smirk. She'd thought that look was reserved for only her. That was something.

"Not just my...my...horse," Harold sputtered. "Everything!"

His clothes did look rather worn...and large... Alys's gaze flitted to Gareth. She'd not been able to look at him earlier, not fully. He'd grown since she'd last seen him. He wasn't just taller, there was something in his stature as the men stood in front of the large fireplace.

"Someone from Ysgarlad must make amends," Harold crowed once more.

Only now did the squire turn their way. "This is no concern of yours."

"We live here," Grandmother said with the same quiet confidence she used in front of all of her father's spies. "We are happy to hear your story. Please, let us sit."

Alys sniffed in her pretend sickness and sat in a chair, pulling her thick shawl more tightly around her shoulders as the men also found a seat. Firelight flickered over the tall walls of the room, the family portraits and tapestries hanging from high above. The entrance hall was not where they would normally entertain visitors. Though, this was most likely the squire's doing, him wanting the castle to appear larger and more impressive—much like his position. In any other estate, any other country, a squire would be just that. Not a spy for a lord's daughter.

"Someone needs to be held accountable," Harold spat. "The last man left on his own horse and had hardly a word to say."

"Hardly a word to say of what?" Grandmother asked, her voice sounding all innocence.

She was a master.

"Of how he was robbed!" Harold threw his hands in the air, and Gareth's brows jumped upward in response, almost as if—was he holding in a laugh?

No. That could not be correct. Gareth worked for the crown, just as Harold.

Harold paced in front of the fireplace. "There is a rebellion in this town, and I will prove it."

"A rebellion?" The squire looked from left to right and then again, as if he expected a band of evildoers to step through the walls. "Here?" Now his tone sounded more incredulous, which could only help the women's cause.

"There are hardly any men left," Grandmother said softly. "And the ones who remain are quite...white-haired..."

At which point Harold ran down the list of names that were very familiar to Alys, as she'd had a hand in robbing each and every one of them. One gentleman came with so much coin, they'd been able to travel to several nearby villages and leave coin on many a doorstep.

Her smile attempted to creep onto her face. Alys immediately mimicked a cough to hide her reaction.

"She's not feeling well," Grandmother explained.

Alys sniffed another time and attempted a meek smile.

Gareth's gaze caught hers and warmth pooled low in her stomach. She should not be reacting to him this way. Not after last night—his nickname of *Wolf* had followed him for a reason.

Two of the man servants stood in the far corner of the room, listening to every word. Lord Gower would hear of Harold's theories from both his servants lurking in the corridor, as well as from the squire. Alys shifted in her seat. The squire was one of very few people who knew Alys's unique skillset. Although, after training most of the women in town, her skill was less *unique* as it was shared.

"I know the people of this village." Gareth stretched to his full height. "They are good people—not common thieves. They are simply attempting to feed their families. Perhaps the tax collectors came back to the king empty-handed because there is nothing left to tax."

While his voice was even and smooth, Alys could detect a slight edge—he was far angrier than he let on, but his demeanor was quiet and calm. This was the kind of strength that would save their village.

"Nonsense." Harold scoffed, his voice echoing in the vast room. "I demand that a letter be sent to Lord Gower."

"I have the Lord's ear..." the squire assured him. "We will learn what is happening here."

"We are simply a very small, very poor village," Lady Ysgarlad said.

Harold's glance could have cut ice.

Grandmother exchanged a look with Alys that screamed, *be careful.*

"You." Harold stood and turned toward Gareth. "I do not trust your loyalties, sir."

"I—p"

But Gareth's words were cut off by Harold. "I will see you hang, boy. Mark my words. There is something sinister here, and I *will* discover what it is."

"Please," Grandmother began.

"And you!" Harold pointed at Grandmother. "There is a reason Lord Gower sent his squire. He does not trust you. I don't trust you either," he snapped. "Someone in this room knows what's happening in this village, and I will not be made a fool."

In a swirl of over-sized clothing, Harold stomped for the door.

Gareth made no move to follow.

Alys held her breath until the door was shut behind Harold.

"Where are his clothes?" she whispered to Gareth. "Surely, his clothing wasn't stolen from his body?"

"He was...sleeping..." Gareth began, his cheeks turning pink. "And wearing only a shirt."

"Ah," she responded. Though, she knew quite well already.

Lady Ysgarlad's lips pursed and to the squire, she possibly looked contemplative. To Alys, she looked as if she were attempting not to laugh.

There was no accounting for Grandmother's glee at the idea someone may discover that women had been besting the king's men one by one.

"I should accompany him to town," Gareth said as he stood. "As much as it pains me."

"Pains you?" the squire said cautiously. "To help a man sent by the king?"

"I was sent by the king." Gareth drew his shoulders back, making the squire shrink in his seat.

"I only meant that..." but the squire ran out of words. "Please tell your...please know that I shall send word to Gower immediately."

Alys and her Grandmother shared another look. Nothing good would come of Lord Gower coming back to Tenby. Alys would need to prevent the letter from leaving the village.

"Lady Ysgarlad, I thank you for your hospitality," Gareth said warmly as he bowed before Grandmother and then to Alys. "It has been a pleasure."

He took one of grandmother's hands and dwarfed it in two of his, and after a quick nod to the squire, stood above Alys, stealing her breath. The familiar lines of his face now mixed with the man in front of her. Her stomach wobbled. Her heart flipped as he took her hands in his. Only...only now resting in her palm was a tightly folded bit of paper.

She clutched her hands together as Gareth pulled away, his gaze still locked on to hers. The dozens of letters they'd once sent to each other, a constant flurry of papers between their estates as children. For a moment, Alys wished Gareth would stay and pretend time had not passed and a war did not rage.

After a few more pleasantries, Gareth followed Harold and left the castle.

"That was most odd." Grandmother shook her head. "Most odd indeed."

"I'm not sure…" the squire trailed off, now seeming uncertain.

"He is a man without his wits about him." She released a sigh. "Lord Gower is forever frustrated with men such as him."

The squire blinked as if mulling over this new information.

"I suppose you shall need to write him," Grandmother said to the squire. "Only, I urge you to be cautious, as Lord Gower is known to be far more frustrated with the sender of information that he finds unfounded."

"You believe the man's claims to be unfounded?" the squire asked.

"I am just a woman," Grandmother replied sweetly. "But he seems the type of man to forget to tie his horse and then blame a vast conspiracy for the missing animal."

Alys curled more tightly into her shawl, the bit of parchment in her palm screaming to be read.

"I'm not feeling well," Alys said in the raspiest voice she could manage. "I need rest."

The squire stood as if to offer a hand to her room when Grandmother wrapped Alys under her arm and led her to the stairs.

"We will converse when you are well," the squire called from below.

Alys didn't respond aside from forcing her body to produce a few more unfounded coughs.

Grandmother paused in her doorway. "I will not be able to keep the squire from speaking to you forever, dear. I'd imagine your father has news."

All Alys could think about was having privacy to read whatever Gareth had placed in her palm. The warmth of his hands. The breadth of his shoulders. The kindness in his eyes…but he was a traitor. He'd said himself, he was back in the village by order of the king.

So, the king must have suspicions to send the mighty wolf to their small village.

Grandmother said something else before leaving, but Alys's mind was elsewhere.

The moment the door closed, Alys began unfolding the parchment. Gareth had created almost a tiny box for her to unfurl.

When the words were finally in front of her, she drew in a deep breath.

Dearest Alys –

Please be careful. Harold is on a mission to uncover whatever he can. He will not wish to return to London empty-handed. The truth is of little matter to him. More important to a man such as him is bringing back a prize on which he can stand.

He will stop at nothing.

While I have not spoken to Lord Gower, it is well known that he is looking for a proper English husband for you. I look back at when I thought I was a man but was still a child. I should have come and taken you in the night. Married you in another village and then at least we'd have been together. There is so much I wish to say, but I will save it for when we can speak face to face.

I have never forgotten you, your strength, your beauty, and your resolve. Please, please be cautious. Burn this letter. If you are willing, let us attempt to speak soon.

Yours,

Gareth

AFTER LETTING herself read the letter several more times, Alys watched it burn—from the outside edges until all that was left was ash.

The easy tempered, smiling boy she once loved was gone. His broad shoulders had carried her into the castle a time or two too many—even broader now, he also seemed quieter, stronger, more thoughtful. Her father had been convinced Gareth was nothing but a dog, his last name meant wolf. Her father used to tease that Gareth should be put on a leash, better to control a dog than wait for it to attack.

But Lord Gower had been wrong about most things in his life— Gareth was simply one in a long line of them.

And now, Alys had more questions than answers. Yes, she would go to town in the morning and would seek him out. But how would she ever find a way for them to have a conversation without drawing suspicion from the women of the village, and from the king's man who had come with him?

One thing was certain. She would need to be more cautious than she'd perhaps ever been.

CHAPTER 6

areth Blaidd

THERE WAS a certain release in giving Lady Alys the letter, and for the first time since arriving, Gareth slept. He didn't sleep long, but he'd slept hard. He woke with a start to near silence.

Silence was good. Silence meant that hopefully Harold was not yet awake. Gareth stretched and quickly dressed before stepping outside and into the early morning light. He allowed himself a short moment to peer toward his family's land before succumbing to the need to step foot on the ground he was serving the king to protect.

In a blur, he was on his quick-footed horse. Not as large as the soldiers used, but with small feet to throw off trackers like himself. The small stallion stretched his legs in a long trot – the both of them feeling a small pinch of freedom—the two took these small liberties whenever they could.

While Gareth was fairly certain about how the tax collectors were being robbed, he wasn't positive. At any rate, he rode through the forest he'd been in the other night with Harold to lay a few false clues. Clues that would lead to villages scattered throughout the area north. Nothing too large and obvious, but a few things he could point to, in order to get Harold off the scent of those responsible in Tenby.

When he was finished, he continued through the woods he'd thought would feel foreign to him after so many years, but were as familiar as his own face. Slightly changed, but also much the same.

Of course the massive Ysgarlad castle came into view far before his own small holding. Though, he should not call his uncle's castle small considering the size of most of the houses in the village.

He hated keeping the place so empty, only a few servants remained, using the small servants' quarters in lieu of their own home. He had not coin to give them, but they had nowhere else to go.

As he drew nearer, he slowed his horse to a walk and let the reins loose. If the world were right, he would live in this house with Alys, be a boon to the village of Tenby, and not be forced to fight on whatever front the king felt the need to use him for.

Gareth was proud of his skills, but there were times when he wished he'd been a lowly foot soldier. Though, he'd very likely be dead by now if that were the case.

Just as he neared the door, the echo of hooves on dirt echoed off the front wall of the castle.

Gareth's heart lept into his throat. He could run inside and hide, slowly draw out the intruder, but then what? If the king had decided he was done with Gareth, there would be little Gareth could do aside from spend the rest of his life poor, starving, and attempting to remain hidden.

He spun his horse around to face whoever was galloping toward his uncle's land. No, his land now. For now...

A familiar cascade of deep copper hair trailed behind a figure he'd know anywhere.

"I thought that might be you," she said easily as she pulled her black mare to a stop.

Gareth's horse immediately arched his head in response to the horse in front of him. *She's way too fine for you my friend,* Gareth thought as he patted his horse. Though, it was probably true for Gareth as well.

"We should tread carefully," Gareth said immediately.

"You said…in your letter," she responded, and her cheeks flushed. "Walk for town? It is very likely that we would share the road given that your estate is next to mine."

"For a while," he replied. "Then I should survey the nearby woods to appease Harold."

Her gaze flicked to his before her attention moved back toward the road.

They urged their horses forward, and as large as her mare looked, she wasn't so much taller than his stallion.

"Where is everyone?" he asked. "There are grandfathers here, and some children, and…"

Her jaw set and her attention remained on the road in front of them. "They all left to be heroes, Gareth. To…to be heroes…" she trailed off.

"For the Welsh or the crown?"

She reached down and patted her horse before answering in a soft voice. "As long as you work for the crown, you know I cannot answer."

They walked in silence for a moment.

"Harold is out for blood, Alys."

She nodded in response.

"Tenby, and other similar villages have become breeding grounds for insurrections. When people have nothing left to lose, they fight much harder."

She released a long breath. "That is why Lord Gower and others like him were called to court."

"That would be my guess," Gareth responded. "By keeping the lower nobility near him, he is able to exercise more control."

"What does Harold stand to gain?" Alys asked slowly.

Gareth attempted to not stare at her slim waist, at the easy and strong way she sat bareback on her horse, the curve of her leg…

"Harold?" she urged.

"The property of traitors...can be confiscated..." Gareth trailed off.

"And Harold has no reason to assume anyone innocent," she finished.

She'd always been astute.

"What were you doing in the woods the other night?" he asked boldly. He wasn't fully certain it had been her, but he was almost. He'd hidden in these woods alongside her enough times that he felt safe asking.

"Who do you work for, Gareth?" she responded.

That alone answered his question.

"You need to be quiet for a while," he said slowly. "Stay home. Be a...lady..."

"I am a lady." She fluttered her lashes at him and tossed him an impish smile. "Grandmother says it would be far better for me to mingle in town as if I've nothing to hide."

And this was confirmation of what he'd suspected since his first night tracking. "I'll part from you now but be cautious. Please."

She could not know how much danger she could be in. What Gareth faced if he didn't appear loyal. He would need to be far more cautious around Harold than he'd been since arriving.

"One day, you will need to tell me what it is...how this all works... Harold wasn't lying when he said this village has a reputation."

A corner of her mouth twitched upward. "Why, Gareth. I cannot possibly understand what you mean. We are all just lowly, silly women."

"Well, that is one thing in your favor," he returned. "The king has no idea the strength of Welsh women."

She studied him for a moment. Her gaze piercing him like it always had. A flash of their kiss lit his mind like a flame.

"What?" he asked, his heart stuttering.

Only the sound of the horse's hooves echoed in the early morning for a few moments.

"Why, Gareth? Why did you leave?"

Gareth watched her strength and wondered if he could fit into her life anymore. He used to be the knight in shining armor, he could reach when she couldn't, he could hold when her arms weren't able.

He forced himself to hold her gaze. He fought the grimace at seeing the pain, the grief in her eye. He had a hand in hurting her. He missed her and ached for the girl she was before life, and the crown, forced her to harden further. She'd climbed trees and do anything to keep up with Gareth when they were young. She would be clutching her sides but still trying. She would practice for hours with a bow and arrow until her fingers bled. Her mother was gone and her father was absent. She was left to her own devices, raised almost entirely by her grandmother.

And now, she rode next to him, most likely the leader, or a leader, of a group of men—he paused—the tax collector had mentioned *little men.* Women. She was leading women who were robbing the king's men and humiliating them to the point that they didn't speak of what had happened. Though, it was likely they didn't remember, given Alys's grandmother's knack for tonics. Alys was bloody brilliant.

"Are you still with me?" Alys asked, a fake lightness to her voice.

"I asked your father for your hand."

She blinked so quickly, he had to look back at the road—feeling the need to give her some privacy.

"I was drafted the following day and taken away."

"Why didn't you run?" she asked.

He did look her fully in the eye then. "Because I would always run. That is not living, Alys. You know that."

She nodded once. "I'll leave you now. Speak with Grandmother."

"Alys." He reached his hand toward her, needing any connection, no matter how brief.

She regarded his extended arm for a moment. Her face flushed, a blush creeping across her face. She lifted her hand and hesitated before squeezing his hand in her own. "Don't worry about me," she said with a partial smile. "All will be well."

But he couldn't believe that—not with so much on the line. Her freedom. Her life. Her safety. His.

In a flash, she was gone, cutting over the fields that led to her castle.

Gareth urged his stallion into a gallop to head back to town. Now he knew. He'd should have suspected Alys and her grandmother from the beginning. Pride encircled him. He grinned liked a fool. He knew how the men arriving in Tenby were being robbed, and all he could think of was how to throw Harold off the trail and still appear loyal to the king.

CHAPTER 7

lys Ysgarlad

THE ONLY THING Alys knew as she galloped across the fields toward the castle was that it was far easier to rob a man than sort out her heart.

Every long stride helped her to sift through her thoughts, but that touch...

Even more than when he'd pressed the letter into her palm, him reaching toward her had nearly undone all the walls she'd built around her heart since he'd left.

She pulled to a stop in front of the castle, just as Lady Ysgarlad appeared on her horse from near the stables.

"Shall we go to town?" Grandmother asked.

"What?" All Alys wanted to do was sit somewhere quiet with her thoughts.

"Shall...we...go...to...town..." Grandmother drew out with a smile. "I saw you riding with Gareth."

"Oh. Yes." Alys laughed lightly. "He was just..."

"Looking for you?" Grandmother urged.

"No...I..." Had he been looking for her? Her stomach twisted at the thought. "I don't know," she said honestly.

"Let us go before the squire wishes to show off his masculinity and join us on a ride." With that, Grandmother headed down the road for town at a brisk trot.

If she went to the village, she would see Gareth again. How could she tell her heart that he was a traitor? A lump formed in her throat. That he couldn't be trusted?

"You must know," Grandmother began, "that Gareth did not volunteer."

"He said as much." What had he said exactly? He'd asked Lord Gower for Alys's hand, and of course Gower would have refused...and then said he had been taken into the king's army.

"His land will go to the king if he does not continue to do as the king asks," Grandmother said plainly. "Surely you've put that together."

No, she hadn't. Not fully. Perhaps she'd been afraid to tell her heart that he was safe—safe to hold, to love. And even if that were the case, Gareth so under the control of the king, was far different than Gareth from her childhood. He was beholden to England.

If her life had taught her one thing, it was that nothing was truly safe.

But still—she felt her heart hope. Until Gareth had left, he and her grandmother had been the two constants in her life. When his uncle died, a part of her heart died as well. Nothing in her life was left untouched by Gareth, nor was his untouched by her.

Her skin warmed with each passing moment dwelling on Gareth. Her heart warming to the idea of Gareth as safe—it wasn't as if their years apart had changed how she felt. They'd only shown her that he wasn't the man she'd grown up with. Until now.

The same Gareth who'd patiently kept her alive—no matter how reckless she'd ridden or what skill she'd wanted to learn—was the same man who would do anything to keep Tenby out of the king's reach. He had not continued earning his reputation as the Wolf because he wished it, but because he knew what the crown would do to this village. And his home.

"I so wish life were simpler," Alys said as they neared the town's center.

"We are all products of the scars we earn," Grandmother said. "You know that as well as anyone."

And Alys supposed that she did. Her life was marked by loss.

"Lord Gower was given land taken from a Welshman and given the castle you call home."

Of course Alys had known that—the inhabitants and relatives were long dead, at least as far as she knew. And she'd called the massive stone structure home for her entire life.

But to have yet another Englishman situated here? Or, since the king seemed determined to keep the lofty men close...it would take more land away from the village.

While Gareth didn't inhabit his uncle's castle, the grounds were still used for growing food that the entire village used.

"How I wish the king were satisfied with the land he already has," Alys ground out.

"In his mind, he already owns us all."

* * *

ALYS AND LADY YSGARLAD left their horses at the inn's stables while Alys attempted to appear as relaxed as possible. As they walked to the baker, Alys wondered why Gareth did not stay in his own castle. Was his position so tenuous that he didn't dare? Gareth was anything if not deliberate. Quiet and thoughtful was how he'd bested her at chess time and again.

She walked into the bakery and nearly turned back around when one of her late-night comrades stood at the counter.

They gave one another a brief nod before she asked how Alys had been.

Their pleasantries were awkward at best, but all Alys could think were the words from Gareth. *Be careful.* Harold was out for blood.

As her and Grandmother walked through town, woman after woman gave them a subtle nod before continuing on. Two men sent from the king in such short order had them all a little...unnerved? Cautious?

"You are acting strange," Grandmother accused quietly. "Someone is likely to notice. Act natural."

As if on cue, Alys stumbled on a pebble. Feeling foolish, she whispered, "The last thing a person could do after someone tells them to act natural, is to do just that."

Grandmother rolled her eyes. "Best go home then. Cough a bit to hold off the squire. Tell him you've overtaxed your delicate sensibilities. He'll love that type of weak, feminine response."

"What will you do?"

"I will go speak with Catrin."

"But—"

"Ah-ah-ah..." Grandmother tutted. "It is quite natural for me to visit with another woman while I'm in the village. Just not with you. Your usual finesse seems to have disappeared."

After their farewells, Alys moved toward the inn stables to retrieve her mare. Grandmother was right, but even as she passed two other young women who had often helped on her night escapades...she could not bring herself to 'act natural'.

Home was the best place for her. Once she had a chance to stand back and put her mind to work, perhaps she would then find a way to be in town while one of the king's men was there and not act a fool.

Grandmother was right. She was not safe until she found a measure of relaxation. A ride home would do nicely.

The stables were empty when she arrived. Instead of asking a groom for her horse, she moved between the large box stalls to her black mare.

"Hello beautiful," Alys whispered as she slipped on the bridle.

She led the horse to the mounting block and grasped a handful of mane.

"You are not being cautious enough," a familiar voice whispered as she remounted her horse.

Alys glanced down to see Gareth.

Where had he come from? Her heart fluttered at his nearness, the words they'd spoken that morning, and what she'd learned since then.

She slipped back to the mounting block, only to be face to face with him.

"You think you are being cautious, but the subtle glances and quick nods are sure signs." He shook his head. "You are smart, Alys. But if this continues, you will one day be caught. And I cannot...I cannot..."

He swallowed and took a step closer.

One step and their bodies would touch. One step and her lips could touch his. One step...

What if he's still lying?

"Why do you..." She took a step back, coughed. Reached out and patted her mare for something to do. "Why do you not stay at your—"

"And give Harold a chance to see what he could confiscate?" Gareth asked. "I cannot risk that land being taken more fully by the king. I am working to earn my right to it."

Alys had been given all the pieces, but to have his situation put so plainly before her... "I'm so sorry."

"I tried to lie another time," he whispered. "Many times, in fact. To help the Welsh."

Alys stared at the ground, letting him continue.

"I lied to save a young boy, and when I was found out, they took the family's food stores from the house and burned them in front of me." His hand rested on her shoulder. "That is why I have to tread so carefully now, and it is nearly impossible while working with that insufferable man."

Finally, Alys allowed herself to peer up at him. She'd been wrong the night before. He was still the boy she remembered—hardened, wiser, but still there. "Grandmother sent me home for my actions," she admitted and hopped off the mounting block.

His eyes lit and he came closer, an almost embrace. Giving in, she rested her cheek on his chest.

Gareth quickly glanced at the area around them and leaned closer, the warmth of him wrapping around her.

"Alys," he whispered into her hair. "I've dreamed of you...I've wished for you..."

She had too—even when she assumed him to be a traitor. She'd wished for the young man she'd known...she'd loved...

"Be careful," she whispered back. "Please."

His lips brushed hers, and the warmth of it spread to her fingers and toes and further tore down the walls of her heart. "Know that I will always come for you. Whenever I am able."

They were not being cautious now. Not in this public place.

Alys forced her feet to move. Forced herself to retake those steps away from him.

"Leg up?" he asked with the same smile he'd had as a boy.

"Thank you, sir," she said in a formal voice.

His familiar hands lowered down, and she set her knee on one hand, and in a quick move—just as they'd done as children—she was back on her horse.

"I thank you for your help in allowing me to better understand the situation of your village," he said, also in a more formal tone.

A groom wandered in and started to saddle a horse in the corner.

Harold's horse.

Her heart thundered. Too close. Far too close.

"As the daughter of Lord Gower, and as someone who has spent their life in this part of the king's great country..." she trailed off, feeling sick just saying the words, but knowing Harold had to be nearby, she continued, "I am very happy to be of service."

"There you are," boomed Harold. "Are you ready to show me what you have found?"

What he'd found? Alys gave Gareth a questioning look.

A subtle wink was all she received in response.

Yes, Gareth was back. And most importantly, he was on her side—*their* side. Tenby's wolf had returned home.

Out of sight of the groom and Harold, Gareth lightly touched her calf.

A promise that they would watch out for each other.

Tears pricked her eyes as she urged her mare forward.

"Lovely to see you again, sir," she said to Harold as she tipped her head in his direction. "I do hope you find what it is that you're looking for."

And now there was nothing to do but go home to her castle. The moonlight that night would not be bright enough for any ventures, which was most likely best.

All she could hope was that they could be cautious enough to send Harold back to the king with an answer that didn't implicate anyone in the village.

And then what? A lump formed in her throat. Would she be forced to say goodbye to Gareth yet again? She could not—would not—imagine it.

She kicked her horse into a gallop, needing the freedom of the wind in her hair—even if only for a while.

But as Alys neared her home, she pulled her mare to a stop.

In front of the castle doors was a familiar carriage.

Lord Gower had come to Tenby.

CHAPTER 8

 areth Blaidd

"Yes, you see here?" Gareth pointed at the foliage he'd purposely ridden through earlier. "This suggests several slight men who moved north after the attack."

"You can tell so much from so little?" Harold squinted at the broken underbrush. He'd not sounded this unconvinced at the other villages.

"There is a reason I've earned the name of Wolf," Gareth said, doing his best to remain relaxed.

A part of him knew he could kill Harold where he stood, but Harold had already sent a scathing letter regarding Gareth's loyalty. Gareth wasn't a fool and neither was the king. He would be blamed if Harold was found dead.

He couldn't risk it—not unless it was his last resort.

"What is that direction?" Harold asked as he squinted through the thick forest.

Taking a bit of liberty, Gareth rattled off the names of about twelve villages. Some real, some not so real…

Harold shook his head. "But the rumors are from *this* village."

"Do you think the Welsh people so daft as to rob within their own village?" Gareth said lightly. "The robberies could also be from other areas, and the broken foliage and tracks through here seem to support that theory."

Harold's eyes narrowed. "Of course you could not implicate the people of your town."

"Don't forget," Gareth corrected. "I've spent as much time in London growing up as here."

"Hmm," was all Harold said in response.

But if Gareth could convince Harold, perhaps he'd gain a measure of freedom.

Freedom.

What would he do with the ability to make his own decisions?

Alys would be first. He would not ask permission from anyone but her if he were to pursue her again. If he could find any possible way to be with her again, he would do whatever it took.

"Let us go to Ysgarlad castle," Harold said as he scrambled up the side of his tall, narrow horse. "Lord Gower is due to arrive today, and I wish to speak with him concerning our discoveries."

A shiver ran down Gareth's spine. *Lord Gower.* Nothing good could possibly come from that man arriving in Tenby. Gower had recently sent his squire, and clearly hadn't intended to come himself. His arrival was a dark omen indeed.

Gareth attempted an easy shrug. "Let us go then."

And as they traveled to the castle Gareth would need to prepare for the performance of his life and hope that Alys could see through the façade.

CHAPTER 9

*L*ady Alys Ysgarlad

Having Lord Gower home was worse than normal. *Father.* She practiced the word in her head like she'd been taught. When she was but five she'd mistakenly addressed him as the Dark Lord, her grandmother was punished. Alys would never forget the stripes of blood on Lady Ysgarlad's back. Her grandmother sharpened her tools for silent rebellion ever since.

The squire stood a couple of steps behind the large man as he paced in front of the fire in the entrance hall.

Of course they'd be in this massive space again rather than a smaller and more comfortable room.

Lord Gower gained a considerable amount of weight since Alys had last seen him, but his presence was just as large. She waited for him to ask her a question but he stayed silent, his eyes flicking between Alys and her grandmother.

"My Lord," Gareth said with a bow as he entered the room.

Alys's heart crawled up her throat, but she attempted to keep her gaze resting on the man who insisted on ruling over her like a tyrannical father.

"It is incredibly embarrassing that the king's men continue to be robbed in the town resting underneath *my* castle." Lord Gower's voice echoed off the walls.

Gareth's eyes widened slightly, but he merely bowed again. Alys hated seeing him cow to any man—much less a man as vile as the one attempting to plan the life of Alys and the rest of the village on a petulant and angry whim.

Goodness Lord Gower knew how to pout. He shifted and grunted in his seat.

Grandmother's lips pursed.

"And what happened to your man?" Gower pointed at Gareth. "And where is this king man? Where is Ha..Ho...Hu...."

"Harold fell from his horse on our journey here, m'Lord." Gareth tipped his head again in an odd sort of miniature bow. "He insisted on traveling this direction in the quickest manner possible to tell you of our discovery."

"And he fell?" Gower folded his arms and studied Gareth carefully.

Alys winced at her father's tone. Wringing her hands, her thoughts turned dark. She willed for Gareth to remain calm.

"His horse, actually," Gareth said. "A servant of yours is attending to him as we speak."

"He will recover?" Gower said, his stance relaxing a bit.

Gareth nodded quickly, and Alys released a long breath.

"Certainly, m'Lord. It's only that his face...well, he went over the gelding's neck as we traveled down the ravine—at his insistence, I might add..."

The ravine. Hope blossomed in her chest. Gareth had played him well. The ravine was the quickest way, but not by much. Gareth's quick-footed horse would have had no problem but the lanky thing that Harold rode...that was another matter entirely.

"And what of his horse?" Alys asked.

A corner of Gareth's mouth turned up. "I am happy to report that aside from a bruised ego, his gelding seems to be fine."

She couldn't prevent the smile from spreading over her face.

They were in the room together. On the same side. Determination set in, strengthening Alys's resolve.

"I don't know that you can be trusted." Lord Gower took several steps closer to Gareth.

Gareth squared his shoulders, and while both were large men, Gareth was far faster. *And a wolf.*

Alys chanted this in her head as the two men stared one another down.

"I have been humiliated in front of the king, lost favor, and now I come home to find you here…" Lord Gower trailed off. "I cannot think this a coincidence."

"Indeed, it is not," Gareth said in a cold and even voice. "I was sent here to track the perpetrators."

"Is that so?" Lord Gower barked out a harsh laugh.

"We have found reason to believe that villages from the north have traversed this direction—"

"Lies," Gower growled. "Your loyalty would never waver to the king. You're poor and dumb and stubborn…just like your uncle."

The only indication of any fury was a quick twitch in Gareth's jaw.

"I will report your falsehoods to the king."

A gasp released from Alys and her knees wobbled. No. This could not happen.

Gower's attention strayed to Alys for only a moment.

Lord Gower took the final few steps to stand in front of Gareth, looking him in the eye. "You. Will. Hang."

"An interesting thing…" Grandmother said calmly as she walked toward the two men. She pulled out Lord Gower's dagger. "How personal a weapon can be…" she trailed off again.

Gower's brows came down. "Do you plan to use that on me?"

"What?" She laughed. "Oh, no…"

Alys bit her lip, stole a glance at Gareth. He furrowed his brow but then a sad smile crossed his face. He'd realized something. Alys looked around, trying to figure out what he knew. She tried to give him a calming look. He might not see a way out of this, but Alys had learned from the best, and the best was Lady Ysgarlad. And while this was their last chance plan, it seemed they'd reached the last chance stage of their escapades.

"It is a very distinct weapon," Grandmother continued, studying the familiar blade in the firelight. "The Ysgarlad crest on the one side. Which of course you had removed, replaced with the Gower crest. One that even the drunkest of men would remember…"

Lord Gower's furious expression softened, as she continued. He was curious. His eyes widened. Possibly afraid. Definitely uneasy.

"And the oddest thing…" she said in a light voice, "is that this was used in each and every one of the robberies. Imagine how the king would feel in knowing one of his most loyal subjects was a part of making him a fool."

"You wouldn't." Lord Gower growled.

Gareth took the moment to stand next to Alys. "Do we need to run?" he whispered.

"Grandmother is smarter than that," she whispered back.

"Here is what will happen next," Grandmother said as she took her turn to pace in front of the fire.

"How *dare* you—"

But she paid no heed to his words. "You will help the village by vouching for Gareth's loyalty. If we blame the scattered villages in the north, we will have time to aid them in causing a great deal of confusion as to who is simply traveling and who is robbing the king's men."

Lord Gower's mouth dropped open.

Alys took a step closer to Gareth, letting their shoulders touch.

His fingers slipped into hers, and as their palms came together, she felt more home, more settled than she had ever dreamed. Yes, if it came to it, she would run with him, but…perhaps they'd find a way to have it all.

"We cannot…I cannot…" Gower stammered.

Grandmother held up the dagger once again, the few scattered gems sparkling in the firelight. "We would bury you in testimonies from the people in this village that your weapon was used. That you cannot control the men in your employ. That your standing means *nothing* here. That the king should have given this castle to someone more worthy, or…"

Alys held her breath. They'd gone over this in case of an emergency, but watching it play out was something far different. And in their earlier schemes, there was no Gareth. Now there was…

Please Grandmother…

"When you guarantee Gareth's loyalty and say how he has helped shed light, you save your reputation in front of the king, and Gareth regains his family's lands."

"I will…not…" But Lord Gower had lost the fight. They all knew it. "I will, but only if Alys will marry a young Englishman."

"And what is your definition?" Alys asked slowly.

"Born in England, of course." Gower sneered as if he'd somehow won.

Gareth's hand tightened around hers. "In that case…" He turned to face Alys. "As a young man born in London, raised half in London, and half in the beautiful wilds of Tenby…I would ask you to be my wife."

"No!" Gower roared.

Grandmother twirled the dagger with the same glint in her eye as that of a cat circling her mouse. "Would you like to leave immediately to lend your report to the king?"

She'd given him an out.

"I'm certain he would love to have word from you so quickly," she continued. "And to know that you have come to see that all is well. That you have leads from villages to the north. That Gareth has performed his duties wonderfully and would make a brilliant Marcher lord."

Gower spun on his heel and bellowed for the servants to ready his carriage as he stomped from the room.

Alys threw her arms around Gareth.

"I meant my words, Alys…" His lips touched her cheek. "I wish to marry you. I wish to never be parted from you again—"

"Never." Her voice cracked. "Promise me you'll never leave—"

"Never." He wrapped his arms around her. "I'll never leave you."

Alys pressed her lips to his, her heart dancing in her chest. Smiling against her lips, he chuckled. She gripped his shirt with both hands and kissed him with the fury of years without him. His hands went to her hair. She tightened her grip. Gareth was here—he was hers.

"I think it's about time *I* leave you," her grandmother chuckled and shooed the servants from the room.

Gareth broke their kiss, his boyish grin on his face. "Wait here."

"No!" Alys grimaced at the desperation in her voice. "Never leave me."

He grabbed her hand and squeezed it. "I was only going to ask Lady Ysgarlad for help in getting us married."

"Together." Leaning against his chest, Alys closed her eyes. "We'll do it together."

ALSO BY CLARISSA KAE

Prince of Death

Reign of Mercy

Reign of Chaos (Winter 2026)

Time Slip Novels

Of Ink And Sea

Women's Fiction

Pieces To Mend

Once And Future Wife Series

Once And Future Wife

Victorian Retellings

A Dark Beauty, Beauty & the Beast

Cinders Like Glass , Cinderella

A Stolen Heart, Robin Hood

Taming Christmas, Taming of the Shrew (standalone)

A Light So Fleeting, Rapunzel (novella)

The Wolf of Heathclove Manor (novella)

CLARISSA KAE

Clarissa Kae is the former president of her local California Writers Club after spending several years as the Critique Director. A stint at Writer's Digest and a Pitch Perfect Conference Coordinator, Clarissa had dedicated countless hours to mentoring fellow authors.

Since her first novel, she's explored different writing genres and created a loyal group of fans who eagerly await her upcoming release. With numerous awards to her name, Clarissa continues to honor the role of storyteller.

Aside from the writing community, she and her daughters founded Kind Girls Make Strong Women to help undervalued nonprofit organizations—from reuniting children with families to giving Junior Olympic athletes their shot at success.

Clarissa lives in the agricultural belly of California with her family of horses, chickens, dogs and kittens a plenty. A graduate of Animal and Veterinary science, Clarissa helms Annie's Aussies, a kennel providing companion, emotional and medical service dogs. She and her daughters also rescue horses, aiding All Seated In A Barn to help 200+ horses.

www.clarissakae.com
Instagram: @clarissa__kae
Facebook: @authorclarissa

www.ingramcontent.com/pod-product-compliance
Lightning Source LLC
Chambersburg PA
CBHW070648130626
46555CB00006B/2774